In memory of my mother and father — M.M.

To Keith — J.C.

A Note on Chalk Cutting

Ever since humans became artists, they have used caves, rocks and hillsides as natural canvases for
their work. There is a gigantic human figure with a serpent nearby in the Rocky Mountains, U.S.A.,
a huge hammer on a hill in Tours, France, and a white horse in the Riff Mountains of Morocco,
North Africa. The world's largest mountain cutting of a horse and rider — the Crazy Horse Memorial —
is under way in South Dakota, U.S.A. and in England new figures were cut into the Sussex Downs
for the Millennium.

England, which has miles of downland, is the home of chalk cutting, with 17 ancient white horses.
The oldest is the Uffington White Horse in Berkshire. It is similar in style to the horses found on
Bronze Age coins and in Scandinavian and North African rock cuttngs. This story was inspired by
the Litlington White Horse on Hindover Hill in East Sussex. Archaeologists say that the horse was
first cut in about 1836.

First published in Great Britain in 2002 by
Frances Lincoln Limited, 4 Torriano Mews
Torriano Avenue, London NW5 2RZ

British Library Cataloguing in Publication Data available on request

ISBN 0-7112-1876-5

Set in Fournier MT

Printed in Singapore

1 3 5 7 9 8 6 4 2

THE HORSE GIRL

Miriam Moss

Illustrated by
Jason Cockcroft

FRANCES LINCOLN

D eep in a huddle of hills, hidden from sight, lies a small village. On the edge of the village lived a girl called Freya with her mother and grandfather.

Before Freya was born, her grandfather carved the most beautiful wood carvings — but not any longer.

Before Freya was born, her mother kept horses — but not any more.

Freya loved horses. The clop of hoofs on cobbles or the clink of a harness in the moonlight were magic to her. Often she lay in the empty stables dreaming of riding across the hills, racing the wind. But it was only a dream, because she never went riding. For some reason her mother didn't like horses, and she had forbidden Freya to go near them.

'Grandfather, why doesn't my mother like horses?" Freya asked one day. Seeing her grandfather's strange expression, she added, "And why did you stop carving wood?"

Her grandfather gazed out of the window through the valley to the hills beyond.

"I will tell you a story, Freya. You're old enough to hear it now."

"Long ago," said her grandfather, his eyes drifting into the past, "when your mother was a child, we kept many horses in our stables. Your mother loved being with them every minute of every day. The people of the valley called her the Horse Girl.

Years later, when she met and fell in love with your father, she gave him as a wedding gift her most precious possession – a horse called Jasper."

Her grandfather went on:
"The night you were born,
your father saddled Jasper
and rode to fetch the midwife, the old
woman on the hill. But there was a terrible
storm. Gales ripped trees from the ground
and the rivers burst their banks. A bolt of
lightning struck the great oak tree by the
bridge. Jasper reared and fell as the tree
split in two, crushing them both.

In her grief, your mother sent all
the horses away to be sold. She never
rode again."

Grandfather looked at Freya. "That was
when I gave up wood carving. Sometimes
broken hearts cannot mend."

Freya's eyes filled with tears.
"Cannot mend?" she said.

Her grandfather looked away.

Freya jumped up. "Yes they can!" she
said fiercely.

Freya tore out of the house, through the village and up on to the hill.

Below her, the river snaked in curves around sheep grazing on the flood-plain. Freya sat down and, through a blur of tears, watched the hedgerows running away into the distance.

After a while she stood up. In the soft grass by her feet she noticed a dark shape. It looked just like an eye.

A seagull screamed in the wind as Freya knelt down and took out her penknife. Around the eye she started to cut out the shape of a horse's head.

All summer, with the silver ridges of the wide sea rippling behind her, Freya cut turf from the hillside. Little by little she shaped her huge horse, uncovering the white chalk beneath the grass. And, as the lines of the horse grew, Freya thought she heard neighing and felt the ground vibrate with impatient hoofs.

Each summer evening when swallows swept the valley, and later in autumn when the long shadows pointed east, Freya covered up her hill-carving with cut turf, and told no one.

Freya finished her chalk horse the day before her birthday.

All at once dark thunder clouds gathered and the hill grew grey. An icy wind tore at Freya, biting into her face. She wrapped her cloak about her, but she couldn't stop shivering. She tried to walk, but her strength drained away.

Crumpling to the ground, she fell into a strange feverish sleep.

F reya dreamed she saw an old woman whose tattered clothes trailed in the wind.

"Your horse has gone to ground," said the old woman, "and you must bring him back."

She pulled something from her pocket. It was a gold ring.

"This ring," said the old woman, "once belonged to your mother." She handed it to Freya and disappeared into the mist.

Freya held the ring. Slowly she felt her strength return.

Freya put the ring on. As she did so, the hill before her opened.

She could see wide chalk steps sloping downwards into darkness. She knew that the horse was there in the hill, for she had heard it neighing and stamping all summer. As she climbed down into the darkness, she started to sing softly to calm her fear.

When she reached the bottom, Freya heard the sound of hoofs on beaten earth as the horse came towards her. Reaching out into the darkness, she put her arms around the horse's neck. Then, taking the bridle, she led him out into the night.

The moon shone clear.

Freya turned, and with a shock she saw that on the horse sat a man. It was her father.

He smiled down at her, then leant forward to stroke her hair. "My Freya," was all he said, before spurring the horse away into the night.

Freya woke on the cold hillside with a start. She stood up stiffly, saw the village lights twinkling down below in the valley, and started quickly for home.

With cheeks aflame, she burst in through the back door. When her mother saw her, she stopped spinning and put her arms round her daughter.

"You're back," she murmured into Freya's hair. "Come on, up to bed. It's late."

On Freya's birthday, a new sun flushed the sky pink.

Silently, one by one, the villagers came out of their cottages and lifted their eyes to the hillside, to Freya's carving. There on the chalk horse sat a man, his cloak flying in the wind. Freya's mother and grandfather stood looking at the man and the horse for a long time.

Freya opened her window.

"Good morning!" she called.

Her mother turned, smiling.

"It's wonderful, Freya!" she said.

After breakfast, Freya's mother took her hand and led her to the stables. She unbolted the door and there, cropping the hay, stood a beautiful white horse.

"For my Horse Girl," said her mother. "Happy Birthday."

Grandfather stood watching them from the house. His present for Freya, carved from the oak that fell in the terrible storm, was waiting for her on the kitchen table.